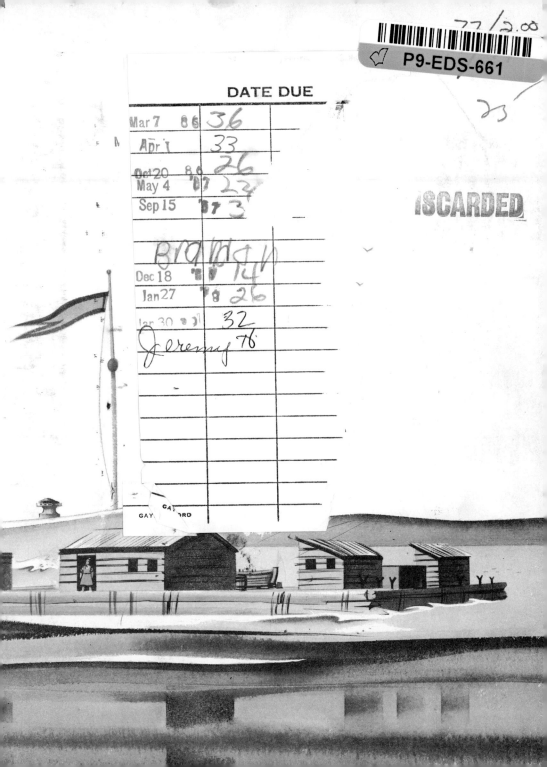

DOWN THE MISSISSIPPI

By the Author

The Donkey Cart
Riding the Pony Express
The Secret Valley
Surprise for a Cowboy
A Ranch for Danny
Johnny Hong of Chinatown
Song of St. Francis
Eagle Feather
Star of Wild Horse Canyon
Down the Mississippi

DOWN THE MISSISSIPPI

Clyde Robert Bulla

ILLUSTRATED BY PETER BURCHARD

THOMAS Y. CROWELL COMPANY · NEW YORK

To
Emma Celeste Thibodaux

Contents

I

Father of Waters

Erik Lind knew that he would always remember the winter of 1850. It had been long and cold. Sometimes he had thought it would never end. But one night a warm wind began to blow. By morning all the snow was gone from the cabin roof, and the Minnesota sky was clear again.

When Erik saw the blue sky, he wanted to kick his heels together. He wanted to shout, "Spring is here! Look, everybody! It's spring!" But he kept quiet. He was almost thirteen now—too old to jump and shout like a little boy.

Mother opened the cabin door. The sun shone in.

"The snow will soon be gone," said Father. "The fields will soon be dry."

Erik's brother Karl spoke up. "Then we can start plowing."

The two boys stood in the doorway. They looked almost like twins. Their hair was yellow. Their skin was fair. Erik was as tall as his brother, although Karl was two years older.

They looked out across the farm. On three sides they could see the dark woods. On the other side was the river. They could not see it from the cabin, but they could hear its deep roar.

"Let's go out," said Erik.

"Don't go far," said Mother. "Breakfast is nearly ready."

The boys put on their wool jackets and beaver-skin caps. They ran outdoors. They slid in the soft, wet snow.

"Feel how wet it is," said Karl. He picked up a handful of snow and pushed it down Erik's neck.

"Just right for snowballs." Erik made a snow-ball and threw it at Karl. It hit him in the side of the head.

"Wait till I catch you!" Karl ran after Erik. He caught him and they fell down. They rolled in the snow.

Mother called from the doorway, "Ah, you stupids! Get up, get up!"

Father laughed. "Let them play," he said.

"Their clothes will get all wet. Do you hear me?" cried Mother. "Stop it, I say!"

Karl and Erik got up. They were laughing.

"We were just having fun," said Erik.

"Come on," said Karl. "Let's give the oxen some hay."

But Erik did not go with him. He waited until Karl was on his way to the barn. Then he turned and ran toward the river.

He stood on the cliff and looked down at the river. Near the shore it was frozen. Farther out, where the current was strong, there was no ice. He could see the brown water rolling along. Far on the other side he could see the woods of Wisconsin.

Mississippi, he said to himself. He liked to say it over and over. At school the teacher had told him it was an Indian name that meant "Father of Waters." It was a great name for a great river.

He wished he could be out there on the water. Some day I *will* be out there, he thought. I'll go down the Mississippi just as far as I can go.

He went over to the woods near the edge of the

cliff. He kicked the snow off a bush. Under the bush was a piece of pine log, partly hollowed out. It was the boat he had started to make last year.

It took a long time to hollow out a log, but when he was through he would have a good boat. It would be a dugout like the Indians made. It would be strong and light and easy to paddle.

No one else knew about the dugout. Mother did not want him to go out on the river. Father would have thought it was foolish to make a boat when there was always farm work to be done. Karl would have thought the same. So Erik had kept it a secret.

He had just pushed the dugout back under the bush when someone called his name.

He jumped and turned around. Karl was coming toward him. He was not far away.

"Breakfast is ready," he said. "Didn't you hear us calling you?"

Erik shook his head.

"What did you come over here for?" asked Karl.

"I wanted to look at the river," said Erik.

"That's all you ever want to do," said Karl. "I don't see what's so wonderful about it. It's just a muddy old river."

"It's *not* just a muddy old river!" said Erik. "It

—it's the Father of Waters! That's what it is!"

"Well, the Father of Waters isn't going to get your breakfast for you. If you want anything to eat, come on." Karl started toward the cabin.

Erik took one more look at the river. Then he followed Karl.

II

The Dugout

A warm rain came. By the time it was over, all the snow was gone. There were days of bright sunshine. Soon the fields were dry enough to plow.

Father put the yoke on the two oxen, Gus and Tinka, and hitched them to the plow. Erik always felt sorry for the oxen with the heavy wooden yoke across their necks, but Gus and Tinka never seemed to mind. They chewed their cuds and their eyes looked sleepy as they pulled the plow along.

"We'll start on the cornfield," Father said.

Karl walked in the row behind him and planted the seeds of corn. Erik walked behind Karl and covered the corn with a hoe.

Birds came flying out of the woods. Most of them were crows and blackbirds. They came to eat the bugs and worms turned up by the plow. They tried to eat the corn, too.

"Shoo!" Karl said, and he threw dirt at them.

"Shoo!" Erik said, and he shook his hoe at them, but they were not much afraid of him. Sometimes the blackbirds came almost near enough to peck his bare toes.

Covering the corn was hard work. The hoe was heavy. The rows were long. By the middle of the day the sun began to feel hot on Erik's head.

"I wish I had a drink," he said to himself, and he thought of a spring in the woods not far away.

He put down his hoe, jumped over the rail fence, and ran into the woods. He found the spring. Lying on the grass, he put his face into the pool of water and drank. And while he

lay there, a sound came to him from a long way off. *Chunk-a-chunk-a-chunk!*

He listened. He held his breath. Then he jumped up and ran toward the river.

He looked out through the trees, and there it was—a steamboat!

It looked like a beautiful white palace with porches and windows. Black smoke came out of

two tall smokestacks. There was a name on the side, but he was too far away to read it. He was almost too far away to hear the *chunk-a-chunk* of the big paddle wheels. The sound came to him like a whisper over the water.

He wished the ship bells would ring. He wished the whistle would blow. But the steamboat moved quietly down the river. He watched until it went out of sight around the bend.

When he came out of the woods, he saw Father and Karl and the oxen in the middle of the field.

"Did you see the steamboat?" he called to them.

"No," said Father.

"It was out in the middle of the current. It went down the river like a big white bird—" Erik stopped. Father and Karl were looking at him as if something was wrong.

"What's the matter?" he asked.

Father held up the hoe. The handle was

broken in two. "You left it on the ground," he said. "One of the oxen stepped on it and broke it."

"Oh," said Erik. "I'll go make another handle. I'll cut a limb off an oak tree and—"

"That's not all," said Father. "Karl was planting the corn. He thought you were behind him, covering it up. When he got to the end of the row, he looked around and you were gone. The corn he had planted was gone, too. The birds had eaten it up as fast as he had planted it."

"Where did you go, Erik?" asked Karl.

"I went to the spring to get a drink," said Erik. "Then I heard the steamboat, and I wanted to see it—"

"Did that take you half an hour?" asked Father.

"I didn't know I was gone that long," said Erik.

Father said no more. He went back to the plow. Erik started to the house to make a handle for the broken hoe.

That night he lay awake in his bed in the loft. Karl was sleeping beside him, but Erik could not sleep. He thought about the seed corn and the hoe. He thought how he had disappointed his father.

Out in the woods a whippoorwill called and a fox barked. A wind blew through the maple tree by the cabin. One of its branches tapped on the window. And always he could hear the river.

He got up and dressed. He thought if he could sit by the river a while he might feel better.

He climbed out the window and into the maple tree. From there it was easy to slide to the ground.

He walked across the field to the river. The moon shone on the water. It made a silver path all the way to the Wisconsin shore.

"You old river," he said. "I'm going with you some day. You wait and see."

He rolled his boat out from under the bushes

and into the moonlight. With his pocket knife
he began to work on it, cutting the wood out of
the middle.

There was a footstep behind him. He looked
around. Father was standing there.

"I heard you get up," said Father. "Why did

you climb out the window and come out here?"

"I couldn't sleep," said Erik, "and I was tired of staying in bed."

Father looked at the boat. "What is it?"

"It's a dugout," said Erik, "like the Indians make."

"What are you making it for? You know your mother doesn't want you to go out on the river."

"I thought she might change her mind when I got bigger," said Erik.

Father sat down on the ground. "Erik, doesn't our farm mean anything to you?"

"Yes," said Erik. "It's a good farm."

"It used to be your grandfather's," said Father. "He came here from Sweden so he could have land of his own. In the old country he was a poor man, but over here he had his own home and his own land. He cut the trees and plowed the ground, and he was proud of his work. He was proud of this farm, and he left it to me. Some day

I want to leave it to you and Karl. Do you under-
stand?"

"Yes," said Erik.

"A man has to care about his land to be a
good farmer," said Father. "I want you to care
about this land. And sometimes you don't seem
to care at all."

Erik looked down at the dugout.

"Don't you want to be a farmer?" asked Father.

"I don't know," said Erik.

"Is there anything you'd rather be?"

"I'd like to be a river man," said Erik.

"What do you mean—a river man?"

"I'd like to work on the boats," said Erik. "I'd
like to go up and down the river."

Father started to say something. Then he
stopped and shook his head. He got up.

"Let's go in," he said.

They walked back to the cabin together
through the bright moonlight.

Planting Song

The sun is bright, the sky is blue, And
The sun is hot, the row is long. I

win-ter's ice and snow are past. It's
bend my back and bow my head. I

spring a-gain, the earth is warm, And
hear the riv-er flow-ing by, And

plant-ing time is here at last.
wish that I were there in-stead.

CHORUS

We drop the seeds in the row—— And cov-er them up with a hoe.—— We work in the sun till plant-ing's done; Then wait for the corn to grow.——

III

Gunder

One evening a neighbor, Mr. Olsen, came down the river in his canoe. He saw Erik on the cliff. "Come here!" he called.

Erik climbed down the cliff.

"I went to the village to get my mail," said Mr. Olsen, "and I got your father's, too."

He gave Erik a letter.

Erik climbed back up the cliff. He ran to the cabin.

"Mail!" he shouted.

Father took the letter and sat down at the table. Mother and Karl and Erik stood around him. They watched while he opened the letter.

"It's from Cousin Gunder," he said.

"Cousin Gunder!" said Mother in surprise. "We haven't heard from him in a year."

"He says he has been working in lumber camps up the river," said Father. "He says in two weeks he will be at Indian Run."

"Indian Run?" said Erik. "That's just up the river."

"He says he will stop and spend a night with us," said Father.

"When did he write that?" Mother looked at the letter. "Just as I thought. He wrote it two weeks ago. He may be here tonight."

"Father, will you let him sleep in the loft with Karl and me?" asked Erik.

"We'll see," said Father.

"Ah, me!" said Mother. "Company coming and my house not clean."

"The house is clean," said Father. "It's always clean. There isn't a speck of dust anywhere."

"Gunder likes to eat," said Mother, "and I have nothing cooked."

"Nothing except a pot of beans and a molasses cake and two mince pies," said Father. "Don't worry. Gunder won't starve."

"But the way he eats! All by himself he could eat a mince pie." Mother put on her apron. "I'll make a potato pudding."

It was getting dark. She lit the candles and took one into the kitchen.

Father smoked his pipe. Erik got out a block of wood and began to carve it. Already he had made five ship models. Now he was making a new one. Karl lay on the floor and looked at a book.

It was almost bedtime when they heard someone whistling outside.

Erik started to the door. Before he could get there, it opened, and there stood Gunder.

Father was a tall man, but Gunder was half a head taller. His hair was yellow and his eyes were blue. He had red cheeks and a big smile.

"Hello, everybody!" he said. "Hello, hello!"

He shook hands with Father and Karl.

"Who is this?" he asked, when he came to Erik. "At first I thought it might be Erik, but this young man is too big."

Erik laughed. "You knew me all the time!"

Mother came out of the kitchen.

"Gunder!" she cried. "We thought you would never come back to see us."

"Didn't you know I had to come back for more of your pie and cake and pickles?" said Gunder.

"Ah, you men! Always hungry," said Mother. "I'll see what I can find for you in the kitchen."

"Don't go. I was only joking," said Gunder. "Let's all sit and talk together. It will be like old times."

They sat around the fireplace. It was not cold enough for much fire, but Karl and Erik kept a few pine cones burning.

Father asked Gunder, "Why aren't you in California digging for gold?"

"If everybody went to California," said Gunder, "there would be nobody left to take care of Minnesota."

"Where were you all winter?" asked Father.

"Up north in a lumber camp. I just came down to Indian Run. They're making up a log raft there. A lumber company in St. Louis bought the logs, and I'm going to help take them down the river."

"Uncle Chris lives in St. Louis," said Mother.

"Why don't you go see him while you are there?"

"I will if I have time," said Gunder.

"I'd like to go down the river on a raft," said Erik.

Father frowned. "I wish you would have a talk with this boy, Gunder. He wants to be a river man. He thinks it would be a good life, working up and down the river. You tell him what it's really like."

"It's a hard life," said Gunder. "It looks easy when you sit on the shore and see the boats go by. But when you're out on the river, working on the boats and rafts, it's hard."

"I'm going to be a farmer," said Karl.

"He's going to be a good one, too," said Father. "I wish Erik—" He stopped. "It's time for you boys to go to bed."

Erik asked Gunder, "Will you sleep in the loft with us?"

"Yes," said Gunder, "but I want to sit up a

little while and talk to your mother and father."

Erik and Karl went to bed.

Karl was soon asleep. Erik stayed awake longer. Voices came to him from the room below. Once he heard his own name. He thought that Father might be telling Gunder about him—how he watched the boats go by when he should have been doing his work.

He pulled the covers over his head to shut out the voices. After a while he went to sleep.

IV

Gunder's Idea

In the morning Erik and Karl were up early. They climbed down the ladder.

"Where is Gunder?" asked Erik.

"He said he was going to sleep in the loft with us," said Karl.

"He did sleep in the loft with you," said Mother. "You never woke up."

"Where is he now?" asked Erik.

"Gone," said Father.

Erik and Karl were disappointed.

"He didn't give us any presents," said Karl. "He always did before."

"I don't think he forgot you," said Mother. "Did you look under your pillows?"

Erik and Karl ran up the ladder.

Erik looked under his pillow. There was a hunting knife with a bone handle and a long, bright blade.

Karl looked under his pillow and found a knife like Erik's.

"This is the best knife I ever had," said Erik.

"Indians made these knives," said Karl. "Look at the Indian carving on the handles."

They put the knives in their belts. They climbed down the ladder.

"Look what Gunder left us," said Karl.

"You see, he didn't forget you," said Mother.

"I wish he could have stayed till we got up," said Erik. "Why did he have to go so soon?"

"He had his work to do," said Father, "just as we have ours."

"It will be a long time before we see him

again," said Mother. "It may be a year or two."

So, when they heard someone outside the cabin that night, they were sure it could not be Gunder.

Not many people came there after dark. Mother looked a little frightened. Father took one of the guns down from over the fireplace. He put his eye to the peephole in the door.

"Well, look who came back!" he shouted.

He threw open the door, and in came Gunder!

"We thought you had gone to St. Louis," said Father.

"Not yet," said Gunder.

He sat down and told them what had happened. "You know we have a crew of men to take the raft to St. Louis, and we have a man to

cook for us. We had another man to help the cook, but yesterday a log rolled on his foot and hurt him. Now he can't go. We have to find someone to take his place." He looked at Erik. "A boy, maybe—"

"Me!" cried Erik.

"Hush!" said Mother.

"*You* couldn't be a cook's helper," said Karl.

."I could, too," said Erik. "I know I could, if somebody told me what to do. Couldn't I, Gunder?"

"Yes, I think you could," said Gunder.

"Do you want Erik to go on that log raft?" asked Father. "Is that why you came back here?"

"Yes, it is," said Gunder.

"He can't go," said Mother. "I don't know how you could think of such a thing. He's only a boy."

"Oh, Mother, I want to go," said Erik. "I *have* to go!"

"Hush!" she said again.

"We'll say no more about this now," said Father.

"But Father—" said Erik.

Father gave him a long look, and Erik was quiet.

They were all quiet until Father said, "It's time for you boys to go to bed."

Erik and Karl climbed into the loft.

Karl whispered, as they got into bed, "I hear them talking down there."

Erik did not answer.

"Mother and Father didn't like it because Gunder wanted to take you down the river," said Karl.

"But I've got to go," said Erik.

"I don't know how you're going if Father and Mother say you can't," said Karl.

Erik didn't know, either. He lay awake in the dark. He tried to think of a way.

In the room below, Mother, Father, and

Gunder were talking. Father frowned as he talked.

"Gunder, I don't know how you could do a thing like this," said Father. "Haven't I had enough trouble with that boy? Every day he leaves his work and goes to look at the river. Boats and the river—it's all he thinks about. Now you come and make everything worse. You want to take him down the Mississippi on a log raft."

"Yes," said Mother, "you have made every-thing worse."

"I don't want to make things worse. I want to make them better," said Gunder. "Don't you see? Erik wants to be a river man, but he doesn't know what a hard life it is. Let him find out for himself. Then maybe he will be glad to come back to the farm."

Father said nothing. He was thinking.

"If he never gets to go down the river, he will spend all his time dreaming about it," said Gunder. "Let him go. Give him a chance to find out what it's really like."

"Erik is too young," said Mother. "The river men are rough. I don't want my boy going among them."

"Erik *is* young," said Gunder, "and some of the men *are* rough, but most of them would be good to a boy. And I'll be there. I'll look after

Erik. I'll be on the raft with him all the time."

Father said, "It might not be a bad idea. When Erik finds out about river life, it will stop his dreaming."

"But he is so young," said Mother.

"Gunder will take care of him," said Father, "and when he gets to St. Louis, Uncle Chris will take care of him. How about it? Shall we let Erik go with Gunder?"

"If you say so," said Mother, "but I don't like it. I don't like it at all."

"It will be all right," said Gunder. "You'll see."

V

The Log Raft

When Erik woke up, the light of a candle was shining in his eyes. Someone was saying, "Erik—Erik! Get up—get up!"

It was Gunder. In a moment Erik was wide awake.

"Is it morning?" he asked.

"Yes," said Gunder. "Put on your clothes and come down."

He left the candle on the floor and climbed down the ladder. Erik jumped out of bed and put on his clothes.

Karl asked in a sleepy voice, "What are you doing?"

"Getting up. It's morning." Erik blew out the candle and went down the ladder.

Mother, Father, and Gunder were in the kitchen. They were sitting at the table.

"Come here, Erik," said Father. "Do you remember what we talked about last night?"

Erik nodded.

"Do you still want to go on the log raft?" asked Father.

"Yes!" said Erik.

"Even if the work is hard?" asked Father.

"Even if you are away from home more than a month?" asked Mother.

"I want to go," said Erik. "Are you going to let me go?"

"Yes," said Father. "We talked it over with Gunder. We're going to let you go."

Karl came down the ladder. "Why is everybody up so early?"

"I'm going with Gunder!" said Erik.

Karl's mouth fell open. "You *are*?"

"Yes!" said Erik. "Mother and Father said I could go."

"Here," said Mother. "Eat your breakfast."

She put breakfast on the table. While the others ate, she made a bundle of Erik's clothes.

Erik was too excited to eat much. He got up from the table.

"All through?" asked Gunder.

"Yes," said Erik.

"So am I," said Gunder.

It was time to go.

Erik thought that he would not see Father, Mother, and Karl again for a long time. He began to feel queer.

"Here are your clothes," said Mother. She gave him the bundle.

Everybody said good-by. Then Erik and Gunder were outside. They walked across the field toward the river.

The sky was growing light, and they could see their way. As they climbed down the cliff, Erik saw a little boat on the sand below.

"Is that your skiff?" he asked.

"Yes," said Gunder.

They pushed the skiff into the water. Gunder got in and picked up the oars. Erik got in after him, and they started up the river.

Gunder kept the skiff near the shore where the current was not so strong. He rowed very fast. The sun had been up only a little while when they came to Indian Run.

Indian Run was a busy village. There were

horses and wagons on the street. There were people along the river. A crowd of men stood on the wharf.

"These men are part of the log raft crew," said Gunder.

He rowed up to the wharf. He threw out the rope and a man caught it and tied up the boat. Gunder and Erik climbed out.

The men looked at Erik. One of them asked, "Who is the boy?"

"My cousin. He's going to be the cook's helper," said Gunder. "Where is the cook?"

"I just saw him at the hotel," said the man.

Gunder and Erik went down the street. They found the cook in front of the hotel. He was a short man without much hair on his head. He had a round face and bright little eyes.

"This is the boy," said Gunder. "He wants to be your helper."

"Well!" said the cook. "Well, well, well!" He

asked Gunder, "Do you know a man on the log raft crew named Simpson?"

"I know him," said Gunder.

"Well, Simpson is going to bring his brother here this morning," said the cook. "His brother wants to be my helper."

"You don't need two helpers," said Gunder.

"No," said the cook, "so what am I going to do?"

A man and a boy were coming down the street.

"Here come Simpson and his brother now," said the cook.

Simpson was a thin man with a long face. His brother was thin, too. He was dressed more like a man than a boy, in a hat and jacket and boots.

Simpson said to the cook, "Here's my brother Lem. He will make you a good helper."

"So will my cousin," said Gunder.

Simpson looked down at Erik. "That *boy?*" he said. "My brother is a *man.*"

Lem looked down at Erik, too. "I'm past sixteen," he said.

"My cousin isn't that old," said Gunder, "but he is big for his age and he is strong."

The cook looked from Erik to Lem and back again. He asked Erik, "Do you know how to peel a potato?"

"I—I think so," said Erik.

"Anybody knows that," said Lem.

"Come on down to the raft," said the cook, "and we'll see."

"Where is the raft?" asked Erik.

"Where are your eyes?" said Lem. "It's right before you."

"Oh, now I see it," said Erik. "I thought it was part of the land!"

The log raft looked as big as his father's cornfield. It was made of thousands of pine logs, all held together with rope and bolts and chains.

The raft was longer than it was wide. At each

end were two small sheds. In the middle was a larger shed with a chimney coming out of the roof.

Gunder told Erik, "That big one is the cook-shed. The little ones are rain-sheds. The men go into them when it rains. They sleep in them, too, when the nights are cold or wet."

"What is the big box on the front of the raft?" asked Erik.

"That's where the pilot stays," Gunder told him. "He keeps his eyes on the river and tells the men how to steer with those oars."

Erik looked at the big oars. There were six on the front of the raft and six on the back. A heavy fork of wood held each one in place.

"Those are the biggest oars I ever saw," said Erik.

"They're big, all right—about thirty feet long," said Gunder. "We have to stand up when we row."

He and Erik walked down a plank and onto the raft. Simpson, Lem, and the cook walked down after them.

The cook went into the cook-shed and brought out two big potatoes. He gave one to Lem and one to Erik.

"Let me see you peel these," he said.

Lem opened his pocket-knife. Erik took his knife out of his belt. It was the one Gunder had given him.

"Ready?" said the cook. "Go!"

Lem began to cut off big pieces of peeling and big pieces of potato with it. Erik peeled his potato so that the peeling fell away in a long, thin curl. He had carved so many ship models that he was quick and sure with a knife. He finished a little before Lem.

The cook looked at the potato Lem had peeled. "You've cut away half of it," he said.

He looked at the potato Erik had peeled. "This

is more like it. You were quick, and you didn't waste any." He said to Gunder, "I think your cousin is going to be a good helper."

"Are you going to take him instead of my brother?" asked Simpson.

"Yes," said the cook.

Simpson was angry. "You'll be sorry," he said.

"I don't think so." The cook said to Erik,

"Come along, and I'll show you the cook-shed."

"Thank you, sir," said Erik.

"You don't have to call me 'sir,'" said the cook. "Everyone calls me 'Cookie.' You can, too."

They went into the cook-shed. It was like a kitchen. There was a stove in the corner. Pots, pans, and kettles hung on the walls. They were not like the ones at home. Erik had never seen such big pots, pans, and kettles before. There was a box full of potatoes and another full of onions. There were shelves with cups and dishes on them. He saw that the cups and dishes were made of tin.

The cook showed him a box by the stove. "This is the wood box. I want you to keep it filled. The woodpile is just outside the cookshed. Look out the window and you can see it."

Erik looked out. He saw the woodpile. And he saw something else. There were men pulling at the big oars. The raft swung slowly away from the wharf. People on the shore began to wave. Simpson's brother stood on the wharf, but he did not wave.

"We're moving!" cried Erik.

"Yes," said the cook. "Here we go."

The big island of logs moved slowly out into the current. They were on their way down the Mississippi.

VI

The First Day

Before he had been on the raft an hour, Erik started to work. He peeled a bucket of potatoes and a bucket of onions.

Cookie put the potatoes and onions into the beef stew he was making. He made corn bread. He made coffee and pies. The pies were pieces of dough with dried apples inside. Erik dropped them into a kettle of hot fat. When they were brown, he took them out with a wooden spoon.

The cook-shed grew hotter and hotter. Erik was glad when Cookie sent him outside to ring the dinner bell.

The dinner bell was an old ship's bell on the side of the cook-shed. Erik rang it.

From all over the raft the men came running. Cookie dished up the dinner and poured the coffee. Erik stood in the doorway and handed the cups and plates to the men as they went by.

Now he could see why all the pots and pans and kettles were so big. They *had* to be big to hold enough food for thirty hungry men.

After dinner Erik washed the dishes and put them away. Not long after that it was time to start getting supper ready.

"You see how it is," said Cookie. "Just one meal after another."

But when supper was over, Erik had a little

time to himself. He walked about the raft. In some places boards were laid across the logs to make walking easier. He liked the pine smell of the boards and logs.

On one side of the raft he saw a skiff. While he was looking at it, Gunder came up to him.

"What is the skiff for?" asked Erik.

"Sometimes one of the men wants to make a quick trip to shore," said Gunder. "Then he needs a skiff."

They walked over to the pilot's box and looked in at the pilot. He was sitting in his chair, watching the river ahead. He wore a black hat, a red silk shirt, and a black tie. He wore white gloves. He looked very important.

"He has been going up and down the Mississippi since he was a boy," said Gunder. "He can look at the water and tell whether it's deep or shallow. Every little wave and current means something to him."

"Does he have to watch all the time?" asked Erik.

"Some parts of the river are safe," said Gunder. "He doesn't have to watch them, and he can sleep. But some parts aren't safe. There is danger of running into rocks and sand bars. When we come to those places, he has to watch."

"Does the raft go all night?" asked Erik.

"Yes," said Gunder, "as long as the river is safe."

About sundown they came into smooth water. The pilot left his box and went to sleep in one of the sheds. The men left their oars. The big raft floated with the current.

Some of the men fished from the sides of the raft. Some of them lay on the boards in front of the cook-shed.

Cookie took an accordion out of a flour sack. He sat in the doorway of the cook-shed and began to play. Erik and Gunder sat down to listen.

"Play fast!" said a little, brown-eyed man.

Cookie played a fast tune. The little man jumped up and began to dance.

"Who is he?" asked Erik.

"His name is Nick. He comes from Italy," said Gunder. "There are men from England and France and Germany on the raft, too."

A young man sat down beside them. "And I'm from Ireland. O'Toole is my name."

"Here on the Mississippi," said Gunder, "you can meet people from all over the world."

Erik lay on the boards between Gunder and O'Toole. He could look across the water and see a long, black boat carrying coal. He could see skiffs along the shore. He could see a steamboat so far down the river that it looked like a toy.

The first star came out, and the air grew cool. Erik lay still and listened to the music. He thought that a raft on the Mississippi was a very good place to be.

VII

Bad Luck Boy

Erik slept in the cook-shed. His bed was a pile of flour sacks. It was a hard bed, but he was always so tired at night that he could have slept on the bare floor.

Cookie told him, "Every night you sleep like a log."

But one night Erik woke up. He had a feeling

55

that something was wrong. The raft was not moving.

He looked out the door. He saw the torches burning—one on each corner of the raft. They were always kept burning at night so that river boats would not run into the raft in the dark. In the light of the torches he could see the men running about. They were talking and shouting.

Erik saw Gunder. He called to him, "What's the matter?"

Gunder said as he went by, "The raft is stuck on a sand bar."

Cookie was awake. "A sand bar?" he said. "That's bad."

"How could we run into a sand bar?" asked Erik. "Didn't the pilot know it was here?"

"The river changes," said Cookie. "Maybe there wasn't any sand bar here a week ago. Maybe it will be gone in another week. Even the best pilot hits a sand bar sometimes."

"Will it take us long to get off?" asked Erik.

"It's hard to tell," said Cookie. "It may take three minutes. It may take three days."

When morning came they were still on the sand bar. Some of the men tried to push the raft off with long poles. Others pulled at the big oars.

Erik looked into the water. He could see part of the long, gray sand bar.

"I've never been stuck in the middle of the river before," said O'Toole.

Simpson spoke up. "Do you know why we're stuck in the middle of the river?" He pointed at Erik. "That boy is the cause of it."

Erik was so surprised he could not say anything.

"How could he be the cause of it?" asked Cookie.

"Because he's bad luck, that's why," said Simpson. "A young boy on a raft is always bad luck. Once I heard about a raft that went down the river with a boy on it. It hit an island and broke up and all the logs were lost. Then there was another raft with a boy on it, and lightning struck it." Simpson was excited. "As long as that boy is on this raft, we're going to have bad luck."

Some of the other men looked at Erik. One of them said, "Maybe he *is* bad luck."

"He *is*," said Simpson. "That boy has got to go!"

Gunder was not far away. He came over to Erik.

"What's the matter here?"

Simpson said again, "That boy has got to go."

"What has he done?" asked Gunder.

"He's bad luck on this raft," said Simpson. "I knew how it would be when we started out. Now you see where we are—stuck on a sand bar."

"You think Erik is to blame for that?" said Gunder.

"Yes, I do," said Simpson.

"But your brother wouldn't have been bad luck, would he?" said Gunder.

"What?" said Simpson.

"I know what's the matter with you," said Gunder. "You wanted your brother to be cook's helper. Now you're trying to get even."

Simpson started toward Gunder. "I'll fix you for that!" He had been trying to push the raft off the sand bar, and he still had one of the long poles in his hand. He tried to knock Gunder down with it.

Gunder jumped back. Another pole was lying by the edge of the raft. He picked it up.

"It's a fight!" said O'Toole.

Cookie pulled Erik out of the way.

The poles cracked together as Simpson and Gunder fought.

Gunder caught the toe of his boot between two logs. He fell to his knees. With a shout, Simpson tried to bring the pole down on

Gunder's head. Gunder rolled out of the way. He jumped to his feet and struck at Simpson as hard as he could. He knocked the pole out of his hands.

Simpson fell backward off the raft. There was a loud splash as he struck the water.

Some of the other men pulled him out. He started for Gunder again, but they held him back.

"The fight is over and Gunder won," said the pilot, "so let that be the end of it."

The men went back to work, trying to push the raft off the sand bar.

About noon a black cloud came over. Rain

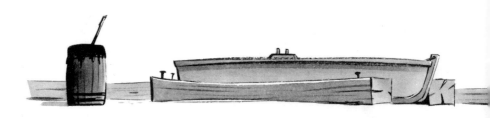

began to fall. The men went into the rain-sheds.

In the cook-shed, Erik cleaned fish for dinner, while Cookie made biscuits and sang a song:

> *Stuck on a sand bar,*
> *Caught in the rain,*
> *We go on eating*
> *Just the same.*

There aren't many potatoes left," said Erik, "and there isn't much wood to burn."

"If we run out, someone can take the skiff over to the shore and get some more," said Cookie. "We won't starve."

"But how are we *ever* going to get off this sand bar?" asked Erik.

Cookie shook his head. "I don't know," he said.

Late in the day the rain stopped. Everyone came out of the sheds.

"There must have been rain up north, too,"

said the pilot. "The old Mississippi is rising."

Gunder said to Erik, "Did you hear that? The river is rising. If it rises enough it will lift the raft off the sand bar."

"Let's try the oars again," said the pilot.

Some of the men pulled at the oars. Some of them pushed with the poles. The raft moved. Everyone gave a shout as it floated free.

They were on their way again.

That night the men lay on the raft. Cookie played his accordion and the men sang. They were glad to be moving again.

"Who said a boy on a raft was bad luck?" said Gunder. "The river came up enough to get us off the sand bar. Maybe this boy is *good* luck."

Everyone laughed but Simpson.

Down the Mississippi

Down the Mis - sis - sip - pi, Down, down, down! A-

way to the end of the line. —

You can take a steam - boat Down, down, down; And

I'll take an is - land of pine. —

Steam-boat's wait-ing Just a-round the bend.

Go your way and I'll go mine.—

Down the Mis-sis-sip-pi, Down, down, down! A-

way to the end of the line.———

VIII

Indians

The next day they tied up at a town. People came down to the shore to see the big raft.

Erik went with Cookie to the grocery store. They bought sacks of potatoes, flour, and sugar and a barrel of crackers. They put all the groceries into a cart and rolled them down to the cook-shed. Then they bought a load of wood.

People came out on the raft with baskets. "Honey for sale!" they called. Or, "Who wants to buy some good fresh eggs?" or, "Chickens and rabbits all ready to fry!"

Cookie bought some eggs. Some of the other men bought big pieces of honeycomb. They broke it apart and ate it like candy.

Boys and girls came out on the raft. They played on the board walks. They peeped into the cook-shed.

One of the girls spoke to Erik. "My name is Caroline."

"And I'm her brother Fred," said one of the boys.

Erik told them his name.

All the other boys and girls came up to talk to him.

"What do you do on the raft?" asked Caroline.

"I help the cook," said Erik.

"Is it fun?" asked Fred.

"Most of the time it's hard work," said Erik.

"Come up and play with us," said Fred.

"We'll show you our church and our school house," said Caroline. "There's no school now, but we can look in the windows."

Erik wanted to go, but Cookie said there was no time.

When the raft pulled away, the people on shore waved good-by.

The boys and girls called, "Good-by—good-by, Erik."

"Good-by," he called, and he said to Gunder, "I like that town."

"Would you rather stay there," asked Gunder, "or go down the river?"

"Go down the river!" said Erik.

The raft had come a long way. They could still look east and see Wisconsin, but now the state on the west was Iowa.

Erik saw dozens of river boats every day. Some

of the steamboats came so close that waves from the paddle wheels washed over the raft. Sometimes the waves knocked the men off their feet. The people on the steamboats looked down and laughed.

It made the raft men angry. They shook their fists at the steamboats.

"I don't like steamboat men!" said Simpson. "They think the whole river belongs to them. They think it's funny when they nearly hit us. They laugh their heads off when they splash us with water. I'd like to get my hands on them!"

Sometimes at night the raft men could hear music on the steamboats. They could look through the steamboat windows and see people dancing under the lights.

Then the raft men would say, "I wish *we* could go to a dance."

One evening, about sundown, they passed a town on the edge of the river. On the side of a building they saw a sign: DANCE TONIGHT.

Some of the men wanted to stop.

"No," said the pilot. "We have to get these logs to St. Louis."

But a few miles farther down the river they ran into a fog and had to stop.

"In this fog we might hit a sand bar or an island," said the pilot.

They pulled over to the shore and tied up to the biggest tree they could find.

"Now we can go to the dance!" said O'Toole.

The men washed their faces in the river. They combed their hair. They put on the cleanest shirts they had.

All the men wanted to go—even the pilot.

"But someone has to stay and guard the raft," he said.

"Let Cookie and the boy stay," said Simpson.

"I want to go, too," said Cookie.

"Erik and I will stay," said Gunder. "Is that all right, Erik?"

"Yes," said Erik.

The pilot lighted one of the big torches on the raft. "Now it will be easy to find the raft when we come back from the dance," he said.

The crowd of men went ashore. Some of them had lanterns to light their way through the woods.

Erik and Gunder sat in the cook-shed. Gunder read an old newspaper by the light of a candle. Erik sat in the doorway.

"The wind is starting to blow," he said.

"Good," said Gunder. "It will blow the fog away."

Erik listened to the night sounds. Frogs were croaking. Water was slapping against the logs. And there was another sound. It sounded like someone moving in the bushes near the raft.

Gunder put down his paper. He was listening, too.

"Look!" said Erik.

Gunder came to the door. A man had just come out of the bushes. He jumped down upon the raft.

"He looks like an Indian," said Gunder.

"Are the Indians friendly here?" asked Erik.

"Not always," said Gunder. "They say the white men are taking all their land along the river."

The man took a few steps toward the cook-shed. Another man came out of the bushes, then another, and another.

"Stand behind me, Erik, and don't be afraid," said Gunder. He called in a loud voice, "Who is it, and what do you want?"

Erik looked out from behind Gunder. He counted the men. Now there were six.

They stood with their heads close together, as if they were talking. Then they came slowly toward the cook-shed.

Gunder held the candle high. The light shone on the men. Their long, black hair hung to their shoulders. They were Indians.

IX

The Steamboat Men

One Indian was in front of the others. He opened his mouth and patted his stomach. "Me hungry!" he said.

"Get some bread, Erik," said Gunder.

Erik took a big piece of corn bread out of the pan on the stove. He gave it to Gunder.

Gunder gave it to the Indian.

The Indian ate some, and the others ate a little. They let most of it fall on the raft.

"You don't seem very hungry to me," said Gunder.

"Meat," said one of the men. "You give meat."

Another one pointed to the sugar sack. "You give shoog!" he said.

He tried to come inside the cook-shed.

"Get back," said Gunder. He shut the door on the Indian's foot. The Indian yelled and pulled his foot out of the way.

Gunder dropped the candle and it went out. He held the door shut.

"They know we are here alone," he said. "They want to take all the food in the cook-shed."

The Indians were beating on the door.

"Can't they get through the window?" asked Erik.

"No," said Gunder. "It's too small."

"I can get through it," said Erik.

"Are you sure?" asked Gunder.

"Yes," said Erik. "I tried one day to see if I could."

"Can you climb out the window and go for help while I hold the door?" asked Gunder.

"Yes!" said Erik.

He climbed through the little window. He knew the Indians would not hear him. They were making too much noise as they pushed at the door.

Erik could feel the wind in his face. Most of the fog had blown away. Overhead he could see a star. And not far away he could see the lights of a steamboat coming up the river!

He ran to the skiff and pushed it into the water. He jumped into it and picked up the oars.

The skiff was light and easy to row. He headed out into the river toward the path of the steamboat.

The current helped him. In a little while he was near the steamboat. The deck lights were shining in his eyes.

He stood up in the skiff. He shouted, "Help!"

The big side-wheel of the steamboat made waves on the water. The waves made the skiff bob up and down. Erik fell to his knees.

When he got up, the steamboat had gone by. No one had seen or heard him, he thought.

Or maybe a steamboat was too big and important to stop for a boy in a skiff.

He began to row toward shore. He was not sure how to get out of the current.

Then he saw that the steamboat was slowing down. It was stopping!

A small boat swung out from the side. It was coming toward him.

There were three men in the boat. One of them was holding up a lantern.

They pulled up beside the skiff.

"What's the matter?" asked one of them.

"Indians!" said Erik. "They're trying to break into our cook-shed. My cousin is holding them off, but there's no one to help him—"

"Where is the cook-shed?" asked the man.

"On our log raft. It's tied up there. You can see the torch."

"How many Indians?" asked the man.

"Six," said Erik.

"Come on," said the man.

He got into the skiff with Erik.

In a little while both boats were at the raft.

In the light of the torch Erik could see the Indians and the cook-shed. The Indians had broken down the door. They were taking out sacks of food.

One of them saw the lantern moving toward them. He shouted to the others. They dropped the sacks and ran. Up the bank they went and into the woods.

"Gunder!" called Erik.

"Here I am," said Gunder. He was lying behind the cook-shed. His hands and feet were tied with rope. Erik untied him.

"Who are these men?" asked Gunder.

"We're from the steamboat," said one of the men. "The boy came out and stopped us, and we gave him a hand."

"Are you all right, Gunder?" asked Erik.

"Yes," said Gunder, "but when they kicked the door down, I couldn't keep them out. All six of them jumped in on me and tied me up." He asked Erik, "Did you really go out and stop the steamboat?"

"Yes, he did. He was out there by the side of us, and the waves were about to tip his boat over," said one of the men. "Will you be all right if we leave you now?"

"Yes," said Gunder. "You gave the Indians a scare. They won't come back."

He and Erik thanked the men. They watched them row back to the steamboat.

"They came just in time," said Gunder. "Those Indians might have taken the raft, too."

The raft men came back from the dance. They saw the broken door of the cook-shed.

"Who did that?" asked Cookie.

Gunder told him about the Indians.

"More bad luck!" said Simpson. "I keep telling you we've got a bad luck boy on this raft."

"Wait till I tell you what happened," said Gunder. "Erik got away and took the skiff out on the river. He stopped a steamboat and got help. Here he came with three steamboat men, and the Indians ran away."

Simpson looked at Erik. "You stopped a steamboat?"

"Yes," said Erik.

"All by yourself?"

"Yes."

Simpson sat down. He put his head in his hands. He was thinking.

He said at last, "I guess I'll have to take back what I said about this boy being bad luck. It seems to me he was pretty good luck tonight. And I take back some of the things I said about steamboat men. They splash us with water and laugh at us, but when we get in trouble, it looks like they're ready to help us out. I guess maybe some of the steamboat men are just as good as raft men!"

Steamboat Men

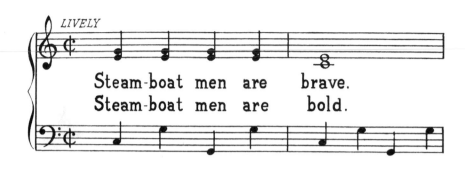

Steam-boat men are brave.
Steam-boat men are bold.

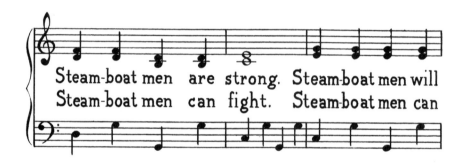

Steam-boat men are strong. Steam-boat men will
Steam-boat men can fight. Steam-boat men can

set you right When-ev-er you are wrong.
work all day And sing and dance all night.

X

St. Louis

Through the warm days and nights the log raft floated down the river. Now when Erik looked west he saw Missouri. When he looked east he saw Illinois.

"We are on the big bend of the Mississippi," Gunder told him. "Just around the bend is St. Louis. The pilot says we'll be there in two more days."

"And then the lumber company will take the raft?"

"Yes. The company will take the logs to a sawmill and saw them into lumber."

"What will they do with the sheds on the raft?" asked Erik.

"Tear them up and use them for lumber, too," said Gunder. "They may send the stove back up the river on a steamboat. Then it will come down the river on another raft."

It made Erik feel strange to think that in a few more days the raft and everything on it would be gone.

He thought, "I'll miss this old raft."

That day the weather began to change. The sky turned gray. The wind turned from hot to cold and back to hot again.

The next day the air was hot and still. Even the river felt hot when Erik washed the breakfast dishes over the side of the raft.

"It's going to storm," the men said to each other.

"I wish we were safe in St. Louis," said Cookie.

"Maybe we can get there before the storm," said Erik.

Cookie looked at the sky and shook his head.

The clouds were black. The wind began to blow. The pilot sent men to the oars. They had to row to keep the wind from blowing the raft against the rocky shore.

Cookie said to Erik, "If the wind blows us against the shore, the raft might break up. We might lose all our logs."

Rain began to fall. Erik had never seen it rain so hard. He thought of the men who had to stand in the rain and pull the oars. He said to Cookie, "I'm glad we have a roof over us."

And all at once there was nothing over them. The wind had blown the roof off the cook-shed. The candle went out. There was a crash of falling

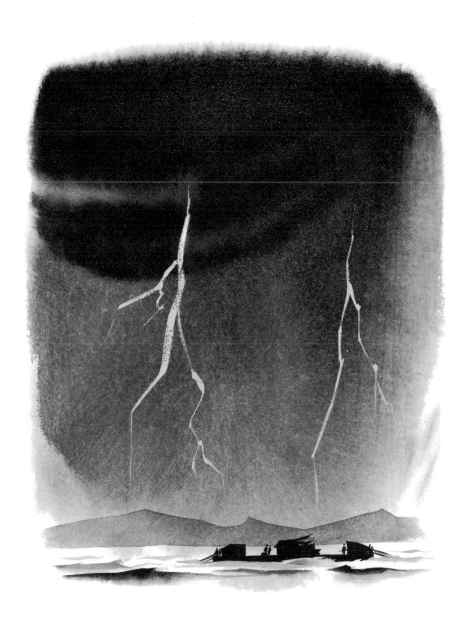

pots and pans. Rain came pouring into the shed.

Erik and Cookie ran out across the raft. They could hardly see their way through the rain.

They found a rain-shed and ran into it.

Lightning flashed, and thunder shook the shed. Big waves came rolling over the raft.

The men took turns at the oars. If they had stopped rowing, even for a little while, the raft would have run into the shore.

Even Erik and Cookie took a turn. It was all Erik could do to pull one of the big oars. Afterward his arms hurt, and he was so tired he lay down on the raft to rest.

"Get up!" Gunder shouted, as he went by. "Go to one of the sheds where it's dry."

But Erik was too tired to move.

When night came, it was still raining, but the wind had begun to die. Erik sat up. He saw lights along the shore.

Gunder was calling him.

"Here I am," said Erik. He got up. He felt cold all over. He began to cough.

"Have you been out here all the time?" asked Gunder. "I told you to get in a dry place."

He led Erik into a shed. They looked out at the lights.

"Do you know where we are?" asked Gunder. "This is St. Louis."

Erik could not answer. He had begun to cough again.

O'Toole looked into the shed. "Have you got a sick boy there?"

"I'm afraid so," said Gunder.

As soon as the raft was tied up at St. Louis, Gunder took Erik up on the levee. Soon they were riding through the streets in a cab pulled by two horses.

The cab stopped in front of a big, dark house.

"Uncle Chris lives here," said Gunder.

Uncle Chris came to the door with a candle

in his hand. He had just got out of bed. He had on a nightcap and a nightshirt.

"Come in, come in!" he said. "Gunder, how are you? And this is Erik? I knew you were coming. Your mother sent me a letter."

"We've been out in the storm," said Gunder. "Erik needs dry clothes and a bed."

"A raft on the river is no place for a boy," said Uncle Chris. "I would not let a boy of mine go on the river."

He put Erik to bed.

Erik had never known a bed could be so soft. He lay there and looked at the room. There was paper on the wall. On the paper were birds and roses. He thought that his uncle must be a very rich man.

Gunder came in to say good night.

"Have you had enough of the river?" he asked.

"Yes—I've had enough," said Erik. The next minute he was asleep.

XI

The Steamboat

When Erik woke up, the sun was shining into the room. He looked at the paper on the walls and remembered that he was in his Uncle Chris' house in St. Louis. He remembered how wet and cold he had been last night and how he had coughed.

He was not cold now. He did not cough.

His arms were sore from pulling the big oar on the raft, but not *very* sore.

His clothes were on a chair by the bed. He felt of them. They were dry. He put them on and started downstairs. On the stairs he met his uncle.

"Good morning, Uncle Chris," he said.

"It isn't morning. It's afternoon," said Uncle Chris. "How do you feel today?"

"I'm all right," said Erik.

"Do you feel like going out for a look at St. Louis?" asked Uncle Chris.

"Yes, sir," said Erik. "Is Gunder coming, too?"

"Gunder is gone," said Uncle Chris.

"Gone? Where?" asked Erik.

"He got a ticket to New Orleans," said Uncle Chris. "He had a chance to ride on a new boat, *The Kingfisher,* and he wanted to go."

"He went away and left me?" said Erik.

"That's all right," said Uncle Chris. "I'm taking care of you now. You can visit me a while. Then I'll take you home to Minnesota."

"Gunder didn't even say good-by," said Erik.

"You were sleeping. I didn't want him to wake you up," said Uncle Chris. "Gunder stayed until two o'clock. Then he had to go. The boat leaves at three."

Erik looked at the clock in the hall below. It was fourteen minutes till three.

"He hasn't gone yet!" Erik ran downstairs.

"Wait!" said Uncle Chris. "You can't go!"

Erik was already out of the house. He was running down the street.

At the end of the street was the levee. It was crowded with horses and mules and wagons and people.

There were river boats all along the levee.

Erik asked a man in a cab, "Which one is *The Kingfisher?*"

All the man said was, "Look out, boy, or you'll get run over."

Erik asked a woman, "Where is *The King-fisher?*"

"I don't know," said the woman. "I just got here from Ohio."

Erik ran along the levee, looking at the boats as he went. One of them looked new. There was smoke coming out of the smokestacks. He read the name on the paddle-box. It was *The King-fisher!*

The plank was down. Erik ran up the plank.

A man in a blue coat stopped him. "Where is your ticket?"

"I don't have one," said Erik, "but my cousin is on this boat, and—"

"You can't ride on this boat without a ticket," said the man. "Get back—*quick*. We're going to take up the plank."

A woman pushed herself between the man

and Erik. She was waving to someone on the levee. "Good-by—good-by!" she called.

Erik ran past her and onto the boat. In a moment he was out of sight in the crowd on deck.

The plank was taken up. The boat began to move. Erik went through the crowds, looking for Gunder.

He found a stairway. It led to the deck above. As he started up the stairs, someone caught his arm. It was the man in the blue coat.

"I told you not to come on this boat without a ticket," he said. "I'll have to put you off at the next stop."

"My cousin is on this boat," said Erik. "I want to find him."

A man came down the stairs. "Erik!" he said. "I *thought* I heard your voice."

It was Gunder.

"What are you doing here?" he asked.

"I wanted to find you," said Erik. "What did you run away from me for?"

"I didn't run away from you," said Gunder. "I thought you wanted to stay in St. Louis with Uncle Chris."

"No," said Erik. "I wanted to stay with you."

"But last night you said you'd had enough of the river."

"I meant I'd had enough of the river for *one day*," said Erik.

Gunder began to laugh. He said to the man in the blue coat, "Let the boy go. I'll buy him a ticket. He's my cousin, and we're going to New Orleans together!"

Gunder took Erik all over the boat. They saw the little pilothouse on the top deck. They looked in and saw the pilot turning the wheel as he steered the boat.

"This isn't much like a log raft, is it?" said Gunder.

"Not much," said Erik.

They went back down the stairs. On the way they met the captain in his black coat with gold buttons.

"Good evening, Captain Korn," said Gunder.

The captain smiled and said, "Good evening to *you.*"

Gunder told Erik, "This is *The Kingfisher's* first trip. The captain is proud of his new steamboat."

"Can we go into the engine room where the boilers and steam engines are?" asked Erik.

"I think so," said Gunder. "I'll find out tomorrow."

They looked into the dining room. There were red carpets on the floor and pictures painted on the walls.

"Look," said Erik. "A white cloth on every table."

"Yes," said Gunder. "You and I are going to

have our supper at one of those tables tonight."

But they did not have supper there that night. No one ever had supper in the dining room of *The Kingfisher*.

Late in the afternoon, when Erik and Gunder were on the first deck, there was a noise like thunder. The boat shook. Erik was thrown half-way across the deck.

He started to get up. There was such a pain in his arm that he lay down again.

At first he thought *The Kingfisher* had run into another boat. Then he heard someone shout, "The boiler blew up! We're going to sink!"

Erik got to his feet. He looked for Gunder and found him lying on the deck. A lamp had fallen and struck his forehead. There was a cut just above his eye.

Erik bent over him. He shook him. Gunder did not move.

He called to the people who went by, "This man is hurt!"

But no one heard him. People were shouting, "Fire! The boat is on fire!"

They were pulling down the small lifeboats that hung above the rail. They were letting the boats down into the water.

Erik went over to the rail. "Help me get this man into one of the boats!"

He could not make himself heard above the noise.

Smoke was blowing out across the deck. Erik could look into the dining room and see the light of the fire. He could feel the steamboat slowly tip to one side.

In the crowd he saw Captain Korn. The captain was helping people into lifeboats.

Erik fought his way through the crowds until he came to the captain's side.

"My cousin is hurt," he shouted. "Will you

please help me get him into one of the boats!"

"Where is he?" asked the captain.

Erik pointed. "Over there."

"Stay with him and wait," said Captain Korn. "I'll help you."

Erik stayed close to Gunder while the people crowded into one lifeboat after another.

At last there was no one at the rail but the captain. He came over to where Erik waited. He lifted Gunder's head and shoulders and dragged him across the deck.

There was a lifeboat in the water. Two men were in the boat. The captain and Erik handed Gunder down to them. Then they helped Erik over the side. Captain Korn was the last one to leave. That lifeboat was the last to leave *The Kingfisher*.

The men rowed toward the Missouri shore.

Erik lay in the bottom of the boat. His arm hurt more than ever.

Gunder began to move, and his eyes opened. He tried to sit up. "Where are we?" he asked. "Where is *The Kingfisher?*"

"There," said Captain Korn. He was looking toward the burning boat. "She was the best steamboat on the river, and look at my *Kingfisher* now."

XII

Back to Minnesota

Late that night a cab left Erik and Gunder at Uncle Chris' door.

Uncle Chris was angry. First he scolded Erik, then he scolded Gunder.

He said to Erik, "See what happens when you run away from me." He said to Gunder, "Why did you let the boy go with you? Both of you might have been killed when that boat blew up."

"Erik was on the boat before I knew about it," said Gunder, "and nobody knew *The Kingfisher* was going to blow up."

"Steamboats are not safe," said Uncle Chris. "I wouldn't ride across the river on one."

"Uncle Chris, Gunder is hurt," said Erik. "Can't we call a doctor for him?"

Uncle Chris stopped scolding. He called a doctor.

The doctor put a bandage on Gunder's forehead. "You have a hard head," he said. "You'll be all right in a day or two."

"Will you look at my arm?" asked Erik.

The doctor looked at it. "Does it hurt when I touch you here?" he asked.

"Yes," said Erik.

The doctor felt Erik's arm. "I can't find any broken bones," he said, "but it's a bad sprain."

He tied Erik's arm up in a tight bandage and

put it in a sling that went around Erik's neck.

Erik said to Gunder, "Now how can I go to New Orleans?"

"You're not going to New Orleans, and neither am I," said Gunder. "As soon as we are both well enough, I'm going to take you home to Minnesota."

A week later they started back.

Uncle Chris told Gunder, "I won't let you take that boy on a steamboat. You take a train. That's the safe way to go."

So Gunder and Erik went part of the way by train and part of the way by stagecoach.

At Indian Run they took a skiff down the river.

"You'll soon be home," said Gunder.

"Yes," said Erik. "Here is the cliff where I used to stand to watch the boats go by."

They left the skiff on the sand at the foot of

the cliff. Together they climbed up the path.

The farm looked different. The corn and wheat were high. But the cabin looked the same, and so did the woods behind it.

Mother was in the doorway. As soon as she saw Erik and Gunder, she called, "Look who is here! Come and see!"

Father and Karl came up from the barn. They all came out to meet Erik and Gunder.

"Ah, you have been away such a long, long time!" Mother saw that Erik's arm was in a sling. "Your arm! What have you done to it?"

Gunder told her what had happened. "And if Erik hadn't stayed with me, I might not have got into one of the lifeboats."

Mother's face was pale. "Ah, what a terrible day that must have been!"

"Was it fun riding on the raft?" asked Karl.

"It was hard work," said Erik. "I had to peel potatoes and clean fish and cut wood. I had to

do everything the cook wanted me to do." He told about the Indians who had tried to take the food from the cook-shed. He told about the storm on the river.

"All these things—they are terrible!" said Mother.

"You see, it is just as we told you," said Father. "Life on the river is too hard for a boy like you."

"Life on a farm is better," said Karl.

"Yes, yes. You will never go on the river again," said Mother. "Come into the house. I will cook you a good dinner."

All the rest of the day they talked. When evening came, Gunder said, "It is time for me to go."

"Can't you stay with us a while longer?" asked Father.

"I talked to a man in Indian Run, and he wants me to work in his lumber mill up the river," said Gunder. "I think I will go with him tomorrow."

Mother shook her head. "Always you are going here and there. When will you ever stay in one place?"

Gunder smiled. He did not answer.

Erik walked with him down the path to the foot of the cliff.

"When are we going down the river again?" he asked.

Gunder turned and looked at him. "What did you say!"

"I said, 'When are we going down the river again?'"

"Listen to me," said Gunder. "Don't you know why I wanted you to go on the raft? Don't you know why your father and mother let you go? We wanted to teach you a lesson. We wanted you to find out what life on the river is really like, so you would be glad to stay on the farm."

"It was hard work on the raft," said Erik. "We had trouble. But I still like the river. I always will. I'd go back down the Mississippi tomorrow, if I could."

"Wouldn't you rather stay on the farm?" asked Gunder.

"*You* don't stay on a farm," said Erik. "*You* keep going up and down the river."

"Yes. I know." Gunder said slowly, "Maybe you and I are two of a kind."

They stood there, looking out across the water.

Gunder asked, "How old are you?"

"Thirteen now," said Erik.

"Stay here a while," said Gunder. "Listen to your father and mother. Work on the farm. Go to school and learn your lessons. You may change your mind and not want to be a river man."

"I don't think I'll change my mind," said Erik.

"Wait a few years, and we'll talk about this again," said Gunder. "If you still want to be a river man, I don't think your mother and father will try to stop you. Maybe we can go down the river again."

"I wish we could go all the way to New Orleans," said Erik.

"We'll go as far as the river goes," said Gunder, "unless you change your mind."

"I won't change my mind," said Erik.

He stood there a long time after Gunder had gone. He looked down the Mississippi toward St. Louis—toward New Orleans. While the sky grew dark, he stood there and listened to the river singing its song.

The River Sings a Song

The riv-er sings a song.— I hear it night and day.—— It tells me of a South-ern sky And plac-es far a-way. — The riv-er sings a song—That no one hears but me.— And day and night I hear it sing-ing,"Come with me to the sea."—